THE COURAGE
OF SARAH NOBLE

by
ALICE
DALGLIESH

Illustrations by
LEONARD WEISGARD

Aladdin Books
Macmillan Publishing Company, New York

For the children of New Milford

who are proud of Sarah Noble

Aladdin Books
Macmillan Publishing Company
866 Third Avenue, New York, NY 10022
Collier Macmillan Canada, Inc.

First Aladdin Books edition 1986

Printed in the United States of America

A hardcover edition of *The Courage of Sarah Noble* is available from Charles Scribner's Sons.

20 19 18 17 16 15 14

Library of Congress Catalog Card Number: 54-5922
ISBN 0-689-71057-7

CONTENTS

AUTHOR'S NOTE

This is a true story, though I have had to imagine many of the details. Sarah Noble was a real little girl who came, in 1707, to cook for her father while he built the first house in New Milford. Most of the New Milford settlers came from Milford, Connecticut, but John Noble came from Westfield, Massachusetts—having bought a share of land from one of the Milford men. The story happened in Connecticut but it might have happened in many other places in America.

Stories like this, of faith and courage and friendship, live a long time and are told and retold. The settlers of New Milford dealt fairly with the Indians, according to the standards of their time, and were always friendly with them.

Sometimes the story is told that John Noble left Sarah with the Indians while he went to guide some men to Albany. I have preferred to suppose that he went to bring—or at least to meet—the rest of the family. This seems more possible.

When Sarah grew up, she taught what was probably the first school in the town. She also married, as in the story she says she will. The records say, too, that Sarah continued to be friendly with the tall Indian who "loved her as he did his own children."

THE COURAGE

OF SARAH NOBLE

"Romance has never painted a picture more perfectly true to the heart of a father, or to the charming bravery of a young daughter only eight years, than is found in the history of the settlement of the first family in the beautiful township of New Milford."

History of the Towns of New Milford and Bridgewater, Connecticut, 1703–1882—SAMUEL ORCUTT

CHAPTER ONE

Night in the Forest

SARAH lay on a quilt under a tree. The darkness was all around her, but through the branches she could see one bright star. It was comfortable to look at.

The spring night was cold, and Sarah drew her warm cloak close. That was comfortable, too. She thought of how her mother had put it around her the day she and her father started out on this long, hard journey.

"Keep up your courage," her mother had said, fastening the cloak under Sarah's chin. "Keep up your courage, Sarah Noble!"

And, indeed, Sarah needed to keep up her courage, for she and her father were going all the way into the wilderness of Connecticut to build a house.

This was the first night they had spent in the forest — the other nights they had come to a settlement. Thomas, the brown horse, was tied nearby. He was asleep on his feet. Against a tree Sarah's father sat, his musket across his knees. Sometimes he nodded, but Sarah knew that if she called to him he would wake. Suddenly she had a great need to hear his voice, even though she could not see his face.

"Wooo—oooh!" Such a strange sound from a nearby tree.

"Father?"

"An owl, Sarah. He is telling you goodnight."

Another longer, louder sound, a stranger sound, as if someone were in pain.

"Father?"

"A fox, Sarah. He is no bigger than a dog. He is calling to his mate."

Sarah closed her eyes
and tried to sleep. Then
came a sound that made
her open her eyes and sit
right up.

"FATHER!"

"Yes, Sarah, it is a wolf.
But I have my musket, and
I am awake."

"I can't sleep, Father.
Tell me about home?"

"What shall I tell
you, Sarah?"

"Anything—if it is
about home."

*Now the howl of the
wolf was a little
farther
away.*

"You remember how it was, Sarah, the day I came home to tell of the land I had bought? You were rocking the baby in the cradle . . ."

"And the baby would not sleep."

"And your mother said . . ."

"You know I cannot take the baby on a long journey. She is so young and she is not strong."

Sarah could see her worried little mother, bending over the cradle, clucking and fussing like a mother hen.

The wolf was farther away, but still one could hear it.

"And you said . . ."

"I said, 'I will go and cook for you, Father.' "

"It was a blessing the Lord gave me daughters, as well as sons," said John Noble. "And one of them all of eight years old, and a born cook. For Mary would not come, nor Hannah."

"No," said Sarah, her voice sounding a little sleepy. "Hannah—would—not—come—nor Mary. It is good—I—like—to cook."

But she felt suddenly and terribly lonely for her mother and for the big family of brothers and sisters. John . . . David . . . Stephen . . . Mary . . . Hannah . . .

three-year old Margaret . . . the baby. . . . And—
could she really cook? She had never made a pie. But
—maybe—you—don't—need—pies—in—the—
wilderness. Keep—up—your—courage—Sarah—
Noble. Keep—up. . . . And holding tightly to a fold
of the warm cloak, Sarah was asleep.

Now the wolf was very far away. But Thomas,
who had raised his head when he heard it, still stood
with his ears lifted . . . listening.

And Sarah's father sat there, wondering if he
should have brought this child into the wilderness.
When the first light of morning came through the
trees, he was still awake.

CHAPTER TWO

Night in the Settlement

The next night was quite different. They came at sundown to a settlement. The houses were brown and homelike. In two of them the sticks of pine used instead of candles were already burning. They shone through the windows with a warm golden light that seemed to say, "Welcome, Sarah Noble!"

Sarah, riding on Thomas, looked down at her father, walking beside her. It had been a long day, and the trail through the forest had not been easy.

"We will spend the night here, Father?"

"Yes," said her father. "And you will sleep safely in a warm house."

Sarah sighed with pleasure. "Lift me down and let me walk, Father? Poor Thomas carries so much he should not carry me too far."

So they were walking, all three of them, when they came to the cabin where the candle wood was lighted early.

They knocked. The latch was lifted and a woman stood in the doorway looking at them.

She is not like my mother, Sarah thought. *Her face is not like a mother's face.*

Still the woman stood and looked at them.

"Good evening," Sarah's father said. "I am John Noble from the Massachusetts colony, and this is my daughter, Sarah. We are on our way to New Milford where I have bought land to build a house. Can you tell us where we could put up for the night?"

The woman looked at them, still without smiling.

"We have not much room," she said, "but you may share what we have. My husband, Andrew Robinson, is away . . . and I had thought it might be wandering Indians. If you do not mind sleeping by the fire . . ."

"We slept in the forest last night," John Noble said. "Anything under a roof will seem fine to us."

So they went in, and Sarah saw the children who were in the house. There were four of them, two boys and two girls, all staring at Sarah with big round eyes. She began to feel shy. And now she was alone, for her father had gone to see to Thomas, and to bring in Sarah's quilt for her to sleep on.

"Be seated," said Mistress Robinson. "You are welcome to share what we have. Lemuel, Abigail, Robert, Mary, this is Sarah Noble."

Sarah smiled timidly at the children.

"Take off your cloak, Sarah."

But Sarah held it closely. "If you do not mind," she said, "I will keep it—I am—I am a little cold."

The children laughed. Sarah sat down at the table, and in a few minutes her father was with them. Now Sarah let the cloak fall back from her shoulders.

"I will hang it up for you," said Abigail. "It is a beautiful warm cloak." Her fingers stroked the cloak lovingly as she hung it on a peg.

"And it is a kind of red," she said. "I would like to have a new cloak."

"You have no need of a new cloak," said her mother, sharply.

Now Mistress Robinson began to ask questions. And as John Noble answered, she began clucking

and fussing just as Sarah's mother might have done. But somehow Sarah's mother fussed in a loving way.

"Taking this dear child into the wilderness with those heathen savages. . . . And she not more than seven. . . ."

"Eight," said Sarah, "though my mother says I am not tall for my age."

"Eight then—what will you do there all alone?"

"My father is with me," Sarah said.

The children's eyes had grown wider and rounder. Now they began to laugh and the younger ones pointed at Sarah.

"She is going to live away off in the woods."

"The Indians will eat you," Lemuel said and smacked his lips loudly.

"They will chop off your head," little Robert added, with a wide innocent smile.

"They will not hurt me," Sarah said. "My father says the Indians are friendly."

"They will skin you alive. . . ." That was Lemuel.

"I have heard that they are friendly," Mistress Robinson put in quickly. "The men who bought the land gave them a fair price."

"And promised they might keep their right to fish in the Great River," said John Noble.

"They will chop off your head," said Robert, and made chopping motions with his hand.

Sarah felt a little sick. This was worse than wolves in the night. Her brothers were not like these boys—and she had heard about Indians. Perhaps . . . perhaps these Indians had changed their minds about being friendly.

She was glad when the children went to bed—all except Abigail, who spoke gently.

"Don't mind the boys," Abigail whispered. "They tease."

But Sarah did mind. If Stephen were with them these boys would not dare to tease her, she thought.

At last it was quiet. The children were all in bed, and Sarah lay on her quilt by the fire. Mistress Robinson covered her up warmly, and for a moment she seemed a little like Sarah's mother.

Then: "So young, so young," she said. "A great pity."

"I would like to have my cloak, if you please," said Sarah.

"But you are warm . . ."

"I am a little cold . . . now."

Mistress Robinson put the cloak over Sarah. "Have it your way, child. But your blood must be thin."

Sarah caught a fold of the cloak in her hand and held it tightly. As she closed her eyes she could see pictures against the dark. They were not comfortable pictures. Before her were miles and miles of trees. Trees, dark and fearful, trees crowding against each other, trees on and on, more trees and more trees. Behind the trees there were men moving . . . were they Indians?

She held the warm material of the cloak even more closely.

"Keep up your courage, Sarah Noble. Keep up your courage!" she whispered to herself.

But it was quite a long time before she slept.

CHAPTER THREE

Down the Long Hill

Now they had come to the last day of the journey. The Indian trail had been narrow, the hills went up and down, up and down. Sarah and her father were tired, and even Thomas walked wearily.

By late afternoon they would be home. Home? No, it wasn't really home, just a place out in the wilderness. But after a while it would be home, John Noble told Sarah it would be. His voice kept leading her on.

"Now we must be about two miles away."

"Now it is surely a mile . . . only a mile."

Sarah's tired feet seemed to dance. She picked some wild flowers and stuck them in the harness behind Thomas's ear.

"You must be well dressed, Thomas," she said. "We are coming home."

She put a pink flower on her own dress and her feet danced along again. Then suddenly she stopped.

"Father, if there is no house where shall we live?"

Her father smiled down at her. "I have told you . . ."

"Then tell me again. I like to hear."

"I hope to find a cave in the side of a hill," he said. "I will make a hut for us, and a fence around it. Then you and Thomas and I will live there until the house is built. Though Thomas will have to help me with the building."

Sarah laughed. "Thomas cannot build a house!" She had a funny picture in her mind of solemn, long-faced Thomas carefully putting the logs in place.

"He can drag logs," her father said. "Soon we shall have a fine house like Mistress Robinson's."

"No," said Sarah. "Like our own."

"And why not like Mistress Robinson's?"

"Because there is no love in that house," said Sarah.

"You are too wise for your years," her father told her.

Now they had come to the top of a long, steep hill and they stopped at a place where there were not many trees, only bushes and coarse grass.

"This is one of the bare places," John Noble said. "The Indians have cleared it for a hunting ground."

Sarah looked around her fearfully. Behind the bushes something stirred . . .

"A deer," said her father, and raised his gun. But Sarah clung to him.

"No, Father, no! Do not shoot it!"

"But we must have meat . . ."

"Not now, not now," Sarah begged. "Its eyes are so gentle, Father."

"Well . . ." said John Noble. But he did not shoot.

The deer rushed away, its white tail showing like a flag. Then Sarah drew a long breath and looked down.

Below there was a valley. "And you would see the Great River if it were not for the trees," her father said.

Sarah looked and looked and filled her mind with the beauty of it. It was a beauty that would stay with

her all her life. Beyond the valley there were green hills, and beyond . . . and beyond . . . and beyond . . . more hills of a strange, soft and misty blue.

The trees were the dark green of firs and the light green of birches in springtime. And now they were friendly. They were not like the angry dark trees that had seemed to stand in their path as they came.

"I do like it," Sarah said. "And I do not see any Indians."

"The Indians are by the Great River," her father said. "And I have told you, Sarah, they are good Indians."

"But Lemuel said . . ."

John Noble took Sarah's small, cold hand in his.

"Mistress Robinson should teach her children to watch their words. She should watch her own. And there are people in this world who do not help others along the way, Sarah, while there are those who do. In our home all will be treated with kindness—always, Sarah. The Indians, too, and they will not harm us."

Now Sarah held her courage a little more firmly. She also held tightly to her father's hand. And so they came, with Thomas, down the long hill into the place that would be their home.

CHAPTER FOUR

Night in the Cave

It was a fair piece of land with the trees already cleared. Men had come over from Milford, on the coast, to buy the land from the Indians. They had cleared it and divided it into plots for the houses. The land sloped down to the Great River, and beyond the river were the Indian fields.

It was in the hill across the river that Sarah and her father found a place hollowed out, that would do for the night.

"And tomorrow I will make it larger and build a shed and a fence," John Noble said.

They took from Thomas the heavy load he had been carrying—bedding and pots, seeds for planting, tools, and warm clothes for the weather that would be coming.

"Tonight we do not need to eat that dry johnny-cake," Sarah said.

It was easy to make a fire outdoors and to stir up a big pot of bean porridge. They ate there by the fire, with the only sound the evening talk of the birds.

Later, when they had gone to bed, Sarah lay looking out at the fire which still glowed in the darkness. It was cold in the cave but Sarah was comfortable. Under the quilt she had wrapped herself in her warm cloak.

Now the night sounds began. Sarah lay and listened. Was she keeping up her courage or was she being afraid?

A branch snapped in the darkness.

"Father?"

"Yes, Sarah?"

"Do not be afraid, Father, I think an owl . . . f-fell off a branch!"

There was the sound of small footsteps.

"Father?"

"Yes, Sarah."

"That is perhaps a woodchuck. It cannot be Indians. . ."

"No, of course not." John Noble smiled in the darkness.

Then there came a strange odor that made Sarah choke.

"Father?"

"Yes, Sarah."

"It is a SKUNK!"

John Noble laughed out loud. "Indeed it is. And a good thing I have you here, Sarah, to keep me from being afraid of all these strange visitors."

Sarah was as proud as could be. She *was* keeping up her courage, then, and her father's, too. That would please her mother.

The night sounds wove themselves into a pleasant, comforting pattern. Sarah tried to keep her eyes open but they kept closing.

The wind in the trees seemed to put words to her thoughts. What was it saying? *Keep up your courage, Sarah Noble. Keep up — keep — keep — keep. . .*

Then suddenly, in no time at all, it was morning and the sun was very bright.

CHAPTER FIVE

Indians!

For some days John Noble was busy making the cave a good place to live. He built a shed with a strong fence around it. He made, too, rough beds of logs, and a table and stools. Sarah took delight in it all.

But after it was done, he said to her, "I must begin the work on the house. It should be finished before winter. You will not mind staying here, Sarah, while Thomas and I work?"

Sarah did mind, but she did not say so. There was still the question of Indians. On the hill and along the river they could see the bark-covered houses. People moved about among the houses, but no Indians had come near the cave. She knew, though, that her father had spoken with some of the men.

She did not want her father to go, but the house must be built. So she looked at him steadily and said,

"I will stay here, Father." But to herself she was saying, "Keep up your courage, Sarah Noble. Keep up your courage!"

Then John Noble and Thomas went across the river at a place where it was not deep. They went on up the hill, and Sarah was alone. For a little while she did not know what to do. Then she took out the Bible they had brought with them. It was a book full of wonderful stories. Which should she read? She liked the story of Sarah, whose namesake she was. Sarah had a son named Isaac. That was a scarey story, but it came out all right in the end.

Then there was the story of David and how he killed the giant. . . . Oh, it was hard to choose.

Sarah sat on a stool at the entrance to the shed, the Bible on her lap. So she had often sat and read to her doll, Arabella, and to her little sister, who never *would* listen. Here there was not anyone to listen—not anyone, not even Arabella, for there had been no room to bring her.

The early June air was mild, but Sarah felt suddenly that she needed her cloak. So she got it, and sat down again.

No one to listen—but she would read to herself. She opened the Bible and there was one of the stories she loved best of all.

It was the story of the boy Samuel and of how the Lord called to him in the night. Sarah thought of the Lord as a kind old man like her grandfather. Her mother said no one knew how He looked, but Sarah was sure *she* knew. She wished He would speak to her as He had to Samuel. That would be exciting. What in the world would she answer?

Sarah read on and on. And then the sounds began. There was a rustling and a sound of feet coming quietly nearer and nearer. . . .

Sarah held tightly to the book and pulled her cloak around her. Rustle—rustle— — — Suddenly Sarah saw a bright eye peering at her through a clink in the log fence.

INDIANS!

They were all around her, some of them crowded in the opening of the palisade. But they were young Indians, not any older than she was. Still, there were many of them. . . . Sarah kept as still as a rabbit in danger. The children came in, creeping nearer, creeping nearer, like small brown field mice, until they were all around Sarah, looking at her.

Sarah closed the book and sat very still. Then she remembered what her father had said as they stood on the hill.

"Good morning," she said politely, "you are welcome to our house."

The Indian children stared at her. Then they came nearer. Soon Sarah found that all around her was a ring of children, standing and sitting, staring, staring with their dark eyes. The spring sun shone on their brown bodies, and Sarah realized with a shock that they were not wearing clothes—unless you could call that one small piece of cloth "clothing." Sarah, secure in dress and cloak and petticoats, felt very well dressed indeed.

The children stared, Sarah began to feel as if their eyes were going all the way through her.

Keep up your courage, Sarah Noble. She thought the words to herself. Here she was in the wilderness with all these Indians around her. She wished the Lord would speak to her as He had to young Samuel. He would tell her what to do.

The Lord did not speak out loud, or at least Sarah did not hear Him. But all at once she knew what to do. She opened the book and began to read to the children. They came nearer and nearer.

They like the story, Sarah thought. *They will not hurt me because they like the story.*

She read and read, and the children listened, because the sound of her voice was strange and pleasant.

Then the story was over and Sarah closed the Bible. Still the children sat and stared and said not a word.

"My name," said Sarah clearly, "is Sarah Noble."

One of the boys said something, then another spoke. Sarah did not understand a word of their strange talk.

"How foolish," she said aloud, "why can't you speak English?"

Perhaps some of her impatience crept into her voice, for the spell was broken. Like the deer when her father lifted the gun, the children were off and away.

Sarah sat there by herself and now she really felt alone.

"Oh," she said to herself. "I wish they would come again!" And she shook her head. "For shame, Sarah Noble, I fear you were not polite. Perhaps they will never come back."

CHAPTER SIX

Friends

The Indian children did come, again and again. Sarah soon lost all fear of them, and they of her. At first the children all looked alike to Sarah, then she began to know each one. Two of them she liked better than all the others. They were brother and sister, a tall serious boy and a little girl with lively black eyes.

Sometimes Sarah tried to read to them but after the first time they did not listen. So Sarah tried teaching them words. Pointing to the table, stool, fire, she would say the name slowly and clearly. Then the Indian children said—or tried to say—the words, shouting with laughter when their tongues could not find a way around the strange sounds.

They, in turn, showed her where the wild strawberries grew. So she went out and filled a basket with

the berries, which were like red jewels in the grass.
When John Noble came home with a duck he had
shot, or a fish caught in the river, he would find ripe
berries waiting, too.

They traded with the Indians for corn, and ground
it with the small mortar and pestle Thomas had

brougnt in one of the saddle bags. Sarah made corn cakes with it, cooking them in the ashes, and all the time she thought of her mother's good bread, baked in the oven. If she had an oven . . .

"I need help to raise the logs for the house," John Noble said. "There is a tall Indian who has said he will help me. I cannot say his name so I will call him Tall John. He speaks a few words of English."

"Father," Sarah said, "the Indian children point to their houses and want me to visit them. Should I go?"

John Noble did not answer at once. He sat with his head in his hands saying not a word. This was his daughter, and he had brought her to this wild place. Often and often he had wondered if he had done right. And what, after all, did he know about these strange people?

Sarah waited for her father to speak.

At last he said, "Tall John has two children, Sarah. I think they are among those who come here. I would trust you to go to the house of Tall John."

"Oh!" said Sarah. "It is Tall John's children that I like!"

So Sarah went often to the house of Tall John and his wife. She could not say the long, long names of the children, so she called the boy Small John and the girl Mary, after her mother.

The Indian children called her Sarah, for that was a name easy to say.

"Sar—ah, Sar—ah, Sar—ah!" Their high, clear voices echoed up and down the valley as she played with them and learned their games.

"Sar—ah, Sar—ah, Sar—ah!"

CHAPTER SEVEN

Keep up Your Courage . . .

In the fall of the year the house was almost finished. A little house, very small in the wilderness, and small, too, beside the great maple trees that looked down on it. The house was brown and the trees had put on their finest scarlet and yellow.

Sarah and her father, Tall John and Thomas all stood and looked at the house. The big chimney promised warm winter days and nights. Outside there was a woodpile, neatly cut and stacked.

"It is a good house," said John Noble.

"Good," said Tall John, who never used two words where one would do—even if he spoke in his own language.

"It is a beautiful house," said Sarah. "When can we live in it? And when will my mother come—and Stephen—and Hannah?"

Her father did not answer her at once. He looked at Tall John. Tall John nodded.

Then Sarah's father took both her hands in his and looked down into her eyes.

"Sarah," he said. "You have been brave, and now you will have to be braver. I must go to fetch your mother and the children. It is too far for you to go and it will be better if you stay here."

"Stay here? Alone? I am afraid."

She heard herself say "afraid" and it was the first time she had said the word out loud.

"I have lost my courage," said Sarah Noble.

"To be afraid and to be brave is the best courage of all," said her father. "But you need not be afraid and you will not be alone. Dry your tears, Sarah. Tall John and his squaw will take care of you."

"You mean," said Sarah not quite believing the words, *"You mean I am to live with the Indians?"*

"That is what I mean," her father said. "Does it seem very hard to you?"

Sarah thought it over. The Indian children were her friends. She loved Tall John and his squaw. But to stay with them, to live in their house, while her father was away—that was quite another matter. And again, Sarah was afraid. But she knew that Thomas would be needed to carry goods when her father brought the family back—Thomas and other horses. Of course there would be no place for Sarah to ride.

The next morning Sarah was very quiet as she stirred the mush for breakfast.

36

"Sarah," said her father. "You will be safe with Tall John and his family."

"But," said Sarah, "what if the Indians from the North come? Tall John is afraid of them."

"The Indians have not come from the North for a long time," her father said. "You know the Indians on Guarding Hill keep watch all the time. I would not leave you, Sarah, if I did not think it was safe."

But to himself he said, "Am I doing right to leave her?" There was worry in his mind.

The frost was on the ground when Sarah stood, holding Tall John's hand, to watch her father start on his journey. Her cloak was wrapped tightly around her. She was not saying anything, but her mind, always busy, was making pictures. Trees . . . trees . . . dark trees . . . narrow paths through the forest . . . wolves . . . bears. Suppose her father never came back and she had to live with the Indians all her life?

Now her father was mounting Thomas. Sarah patted the horse's nose. His long, solemn face seemed suddenly very dear to her.

John Noble rode quickly away—turning once, twice, three times to wave to a very small girl in a red-brown cloak.

Keep up your courage, Sarah Noble.

Now he was far away—farther away. The trees hid him and he was out of sight.

Keep up your courage, Sarah Noble.

Sarah's fingers were cold in Tall John's hand and the tears she had been holding back splashed on her cloak. Tall John swung her up on his shoulder. Then they went, with long strides, down the hill, across the river, to Tall John's house.

CHAPTER EIGHT

In the Indian House

The first night was the strangest. All day Sarah had played with the children. They did not speak in the same words but somehow they understood each other. When they couldn't understand it did not seem to matter. Friends have ways of speaking without words.

But darkness came early, and Sarah found herself in the house with Tall John and his family. How she longed for her own family! The evening meal was not what Sarah was used to. The Indians ate with their hands and they had no plates. Still, the meat tasted good, and Tall John's wife had cooked it. Sarah liked cooking, but there were times when she tired of it. So she ate the food and enjoyed it.

When bedtime came, Sarah opened the bag she had packed so neatly—the bag that had come all the way from home on the willing back of Thomas. The children watched eagerly. What magic was Sarah going to take out of the bag? But there was no magic, only a long warm nightgown and a comb. The children watched, interested but puzzled, as Sarah put on the nightgown. Their eyes never left her as she combed out her long hair. That long, brown hair of Sarah's—it was like the silk on the corn in late summer. The children came near and touched it.

Then Sarah knelt by the side of the low bed covered with furs, to say her prayers as she always did. She said them aloud as she had done when her father was there to listen. The tears came again, for it was a lonely business.

"God bless my father and my mother and my brothers and sisters. Make the baby strong and well. Keep—keep my father—safe—and bring him back to me. . ."

She stopped for a minute, partly because her voice was choked, but partly because she did not know if it was right to pray for a horse. Then she went on:

"And keep Thomas safe on the way. And keep me safe . . . and . . ."

Now she really had to
stop and think. Was it right
to pray for Indians? Did the
Lord take care of Indians?
She could only ask Him
and see. . .

"Please, God, if you take
care of the Indians, too, bless
Tall John, and his wife and
Small John and Mary. For
ever and ever. Amen."

The children heard their
names and looked at their
father with a question in
their eyes.

"She speaks with her
Great Spirit," their father said.
"As we speak with our Great
Spirit."

"Good," said Small John,
who was like his father in not
wasting words.

CHAPTER NINE

Night of Fear

October days were warm and sunny. The Indian women spread the corn out to dry. At night Sarah helped them to cover it carefully, so the heavy dew would not wet it.

There were many things to do. Tall John's wife taught Sarah how to weave a basket. And because Sarah's clothes were stiff and heavy, the Indian woman made her clothes of deerskin, such as the Indians wore when the days grew colder. She also made a pair of deerskin moccasins. Sarah's feet felt light and free; she walked softly as the Indian children did.

Often she thought of her family. Were they on the way? Would Hannah and Margaret be afraid of wolves? Stephen would not be. And the baby was too young to know about the danger. . .

There was nothing, she thought, to be afraid of here with Tall John and his family. But there *was*.

The pleasant, quiet days came to an end, and all at once Sarah felt that there was fear and disturbance in the air. More Indians kept watch on Guarding Hill. The Indians from the North must be coming.

So Sarah scarcely knew whether to sleep at night. Suppose. . . Suppose. . . But tired from long days in the sun she slept at last, always with a fold of her cloak caught in her hand. And before she slept she said to herself:

Keep up your courage, Sarah Noble. Keep up your courage.

Once in the night she wakened and listened. Tall John had told her, partly in words and partly by signs, that all along the Great River there were hills like Guarding Hill, where men kept watch. If the Indians from the North were coming, the word would be passed from hill to hill by calling—and the villages would be ready.

Sarah listened and listened. Once she seemed to hear a long, low wailing.

Was this the signal? Were the Indians coming down from the North? She waited for the village to waken, but everything was still. In the darkness she could hear the even sleep-breathing of Tall John and his wife, of Small John and Mary.

"Why, it's nothing but a wolf!" said Sarah. Soon her heart beat quietly and she, too, was breathing evenly in sleep.

In the morning Tall John told her that there had been fear—but the danger had passed. The river villages would not be raided.

So forgetting all her fears of the night before, Sarah played with the other children. It was such a charming game they played in the warm sunshine. Taking off all their moccasins they placed them in a row, then hid a pebble in one. Sarah was pleased when it came her turn to guess — and she guessed right. The pebble was in her own shoe! In the middle of the game she turned suddenly, feeling that someone was watching her.

And it was her father! John Noble stood there, saying not a word. His eyes crinkled up at the corners the way they did when he was amused, and he said, "Sarah! I had thought you were one of the Indian children!"

"Father!" said Sarah, and ran to him. "Has my mother come?"

"We are all here, now," said her father. "I have come to take you home. But, daughter, I think it would be well to put on your own clothes, or your mother will surely not know you!"

So Sarah put on her clothes, piece by stiff piece. She now thought of buttons as tiresome, and as for petticoats . . . The moccasins she kept on, for her feet refused to go into those heavy leather shoes. When she was ready to leave, she saw Tall John looking sadly at her.

"You go . . . Sarah . . ." he said.

"I must," said Sarah. "My mother is here."

Tall John said nothing, but swung Sarah up on his shoulder, as he had done many times before.

CHAPTER TEN

Sarah Goes Home

Over the river they went, with Sarah riding on Tall John's shoulder. Once—only once—she looked back at the Indian house. They had been kind to her, but now she was going home.

The words sounded so fine that she said them over and over to herself as Tall John waded carefully through the water.

Going home—going home—going home—

Would her mother know her—tall and sun-browned? Would baby Mabel know her? Had Mabel grown? Was she stronger? She had been such a fretful, sickly baby...

Now they were going up the hill and the brown log house was in sight. There was someone standing in the doorway, someone in a blue dress. Yes, it was her mother, it really and truly was Sarah's mother,

and—yes—she was holding the baby in her arms!

Beside her were Stephen and Mary—and Hannah— and little Margaret. Sarah almost jumped from Tall John's shoulder.

"Easy, now, Sarah," her father said. "You will be there soon enough."

Hurry, Tall John, hurry. Take longer steps. Hurry, Tall John, my mother is waiting!

Tall John, feeling the quivers of excitement that raced through Sarah's body, set her down.

"You go, now," he said. "My daughter." Then he turned and went back toward his own house. And Sarah walked swiftly and softly to her home.

Her mother had put the baby on the ground. Wonder of wonders—Mabel was taking a few unsteady steps, holding her mother's hands! Sarah knelt and held out her arms and the baby came into them. Sarah could feel the little body, firm and strong. If the baby had taken the long journey earlier it might not have been that way.

Now Sarah's mother held them both close to her.

"Sarah, Sarah! How you have grown, child! How brown you are!" And in the same breath, "What are those outlandish things you are wearing on your feet?"

Now Sarah *knew* that she was home!

It was a day of happiness and of work for the family. There were goods to be unpacked and places to be found for them. Thomas had brought Sarah's own little stool—she carried it at once to the fireplace.

"Mother," she said, almost afraid to ask the question. "Did you bring Arabella? Or was there no room for her?"

"She is here," her mother said. "We could not leave her behind. Though, to be sure, I thought you might have outgrown her, and she might be for Margaret."

"Arabella is my child," said Sarah. "And I have not outgrown her."

CHAPTER ELEVEN

Night in the Log House

In the evening, when the baby and Margaret were asleep, Sarah, her mother and father and the older children sat by the fire. It was warm and cozy in the little house.

"I cannot think," Sarah's mother said, "how your father could leave you alone with those savages. I had words with him when he came."

"But they are *not* savages," Sarah said. "They are our friends and Tall John's wife takes good care of her children."

"Indeed," said John Noble, "that is true. And when I came back I found Sarah as clean and—and— well-dressed as when I left her. Tall John's wife is almost as careful as you, Mary."

Sarah's mother did not believe a word of it. *That* she would have to see for herself—if she could even bring herself to look into one of those queer wig-wams. No Indian mother could be as good a mother as she was. And certainly not as good a housekeeper.

"I must put Arabella to bed," said Sarah. They could hear her talking to the doll.

"Do not be afraid, Arabella," she said. "It is safe here. These Indians are our friends and they will tell us if the Indians from the North are coming. Sleep well, my dear. Keep up your courage, Arabella, keep up your courage."

Sarah's father smiled at her mother.

"It is good," he said, "to see that Sarah is a little girl again. She has had, in these months to be too much of a woman."

Sarah, hearing, came back. "I am not a little girl now," she said, stretching to her full height. "See, I am tall, and almost nine years old, nearly a woman."

"And so you are," her mother told her.

"When I am a grown woman," Sarah said, "I shall be a mother and have twelve children. And maybe," she added, "I will be a school teacher. I taught the Indian children. . ."

"We shall see," her mother said. "But if you are to be a teacher, you will have to start again with your reading and writing. And, Sarah, it is time for bed."

There had been nights when Sarah had not liked to hear the words "time for bed." Now she loved the sound of her mother's voice saying them.

That night Sarah slept warm under the quilts. On a peg near by hung her cloak—and she did not need it. She had kept up her courage and it was something that would be always with her. Always—even when the cloak was all worn out.

Tonight the pictures in her mind were comfortable ones—home—family—the fireside and a door securely fastened. The light from the fire made pleasant patterns in the darkness. Sarah lay quietly, and the wind in the trees sang her to sleep.